The House That Shlomo Built

by RUTH ZAKUTINSKY

Illustrated by Albert Hakakian

The land of Israel had a new king.

His name was Shlomo, the son of King David.

Shlomo's name means peace, and Shlomo lived in peace with all his neighbors.

King Shlomo was also the wisest of all men. He even understood the language of all the animals.

Shlomo wanted to build the Bais HaMikdash — a special House for HaShem — on Mt. Moriah in Jerusalem. His father, King David, had bought the land for this special House with money collected from all the people. Here would be everyone's House of love and prayer to HaShem.

1) Find the card with the picture of the Menorah & Oil.
Put it on the box with the number 1.

The field on Mt. Moriah had once been owned by two brothers. Each lived in a house on opposite sides of the mountain. They worked the land together, and when they gathered in the harvest, they divided their crop equally.

One brother was married and had many children. He lay in bed awake at night thinking, "Why do I need so much of the wheat we harvested? My poor brother has no wife or children and must be lonely. Let him at least have more worldly riches." With this in mind, he picked up a huge bundle to bring to his brother's barn.

At the same time, the unmarried brother was lying awake and thinking, "Why do I need so much of the crop? My brother has a big family to take care of, and could use more wheat. I can get along very well with less."

The two brothers each left their houses with the wheat to bring to the other. As they saw each other, they began to run with the gifts they had meant to give secretly. Neither had to say anything, and they hugged in brotherly love.

It was on this field of brotherly love, on Mt. Moriah, that Shlomo's father, King David, had begun preparing for the building of the Bais HaMikdash. He even dug the basement with underground tunnels. But, King David could not build the Bais HaMikdash. He had been a soldier, fighting to get all the wicked people out of the land of Israel. He could not build a House that would represent peace for the whole world.

And so he gave Shlomo the special scroll with the plans of the Holy Temple. Shlomo looked at the scroll. There was so much to do to build the Bais HaMikdash. And so many things he would need, like stone, wood, copper, and gold.

The stones he needed were a special problem to King Shlomo. No hammers, axes, or any tools made of iron could be used to cut the stone. "Iron tools are used in war," said Shlomo, "but HaShem's House is a house of peace."

What could be used instead of iron tools to cut through a mountain and get the stones the exact size needed? Shlomo thought and thought. "I know! The Shamir!" Shlomo exclaimed at last. Many years before when HaShem had created the world, He created a special, tiny worm called the Shamir. This unusual worm can cut all types of stone, and it is so strong it can split a mountain.

Shlomo called his pet eagle, the king of all birds, and sent him to bring the Shamir from the Garden of Eden, where the Shamir had been waiting all these years. The eagle lifted its wings and flew swiftly from the palace to the Garden of Eden. There he found the Shamir, and he brought it to Shlomo.

2) Find the card with the picture of the *Mizbayach* — Altar.
Put it on the box with the number 2.

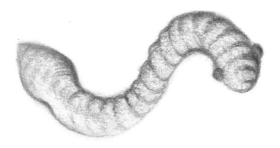

Shlomo took the Shamir to the mountains of Jerusalem. The tiny worm crawled along the mountain, carving out limestone blocks as tall as a man and as heavy as ten elephants.

3) Find the card with the picture of the *Shulchan* — Table, and *Challahs* — Put it on the box with the number 3.

Thousands of workers carried these enormous stones down the mountains. The gigantic stones seemed as light as pillows; it was as if they were carrying themselves. As the men travelled down the steep mountain slopes, no one tripped and no one fell. No one even scraped his finger while Shlomo's House for HaShem was being built.

4) Find the card with the picture of the *Kiyor* —
Laver for washing hands.
Put it on the box with the number 4.

Now that he had the stone, Shlomo needed the wood. What kind could Shlomo use to build the Bais HaMikdash? "The tall strong trees that grow in Lebanon are perfect for the walls," said Shlomo. But how would they get the trees to Jerusalem?

5) Find the card with the picture of the *Aron HaKodesh* — Holy Ark. Put it on the box with the number 5.

King Hiram of Tyre was a good friend. He wanted to help. "I will send my special wood cutters into the forests to cut down the cedar trees. And we will tie the trees together to make rafts. Then the rafts will float on the sea like ships."

Shlomo's workers waited, till in the distance they saw the trees sailing to Israel's shore. They untied the wood and carried each tree up the hills to Jerusalem.

"A house needs windows," said Shlomo. "This House needs special windows because the holiness of HaShem's light must shine out and light up the whole world." So in the House that Shlomo built, the windows opened wide to the outside.

6) Find the card with the picture of the Musical Instruments. Put it on the box with the number 6.

7) Find the card with the picture of the High Priest's clothes.
   Put it on the box with the number 7.

All the people in the land of Israel wanted to help build the Bais HaMikdash for HaShem, so everyone gave money to build the walls.

The poor people were the last to send in their money because they had so little. Their money came just in time to build the Western Wall. This Western Wall is the only Wall we have today. It is our special connection to HaShem.

8) Find the card with the picture of the *Luchos* — Ten Commandments and Torah Scroll.
Put it on the box with the number 8.

9) Find the card with the picture of the Tzedaka box.
   Put it on the box with the number 9.

After seven years, the House that Shlomo built was finished. It was more beautiful than anyone could have imagined. Now King Shlomo could finally bring the Holy Ark and the Torah to its special place in the Bais HaMikdash where they could stay forever. All the people of Israel gathered together, rejoicing. They stayed to celebrate for two whole weeks.

The people loved the House very much. They came from everywhere in the land of Israel at least three times a year to pray and bring presents to HaShem in the House that Shlomo built.

In later years, when the Jewish people moved to other places throughout the world, they built synagogues like Shlomo's Bais HaMikdash wherever they lived, so they, too, could honor and worship HaShem.

These Houses for Hashem always faced the direction of Jerusalem, and the people never forgot the House that Shlomo built.

And to this very day they pray, "May the Bais HaMikdash be rebuilt speedily in our day."

Turn the cards over, one at a time, to make a surprise picture.

The House That Shlomo Built

Hebrew words and their meanings:

Shlomo is Hebrew for Solomon.

Bais HaMikdash is the Holy Temple that once stood in Jerusalem.

HaShem is the Hebrew word in place of G-d.

Aron HaKodesh is the Holy Ark where the Torah is kept.